First published 2006 by Walker Books Ltd
87 Vauxhall Walk, London SE11 5HJ

10 9 8 7 6 5 4 3 2 1

This book has been typeset in ITC Kabel

Printed in China

British Library Cataloguing in Publication Data:
a catalogue record for this book is available from
the British Library

ISBN-13: 978-1-84428-738-3
ISBN-10: 1-84428-738-6

www.walkerbooks.co.uk

WALKER BOOKS
AND SUBSIDIARIES
LONDON • BOSTON • SYDNEY • AUCKLAND

For Annie
G.W.

The author and publisher would like
to thank Sue Ellis at the Centre for Literacy in
Primary Education, Martin Jenkins and Paul Harrison
for their invaluable input and guidance
during the making of this book.

OSCAR and the MOTH

A BOOK ABOUT LIGHT AND DARK

Geoff Waring

One summer evening, Oscar lay on the warm back step.

Moth was just waking up.
"Where does the sun go at night?" Oscar asked her.
"It doesn't go anywhere," Moth answered, "but the Earth is always turning round. Now it's turning slowly away from the sun."

Oscar was surprised.
"I'm not turning round!" he said.

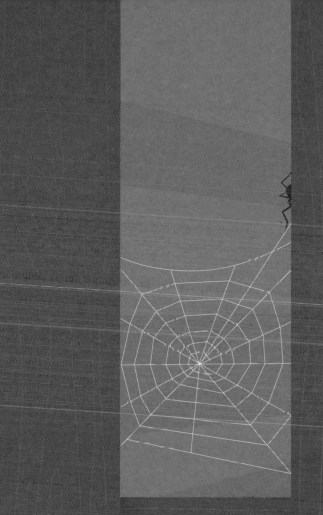

"We can't feel it," Moth said, "but we can see it. When our side of the Earth turns towards the sun, it gets light. And when it turns away again, it gets dark."

MORNING

LUNCHTIME

EVENING

Oscar sat up. "I'm cold," he shivered.

"It's because we've turned away
from the sun," said Moth, "and
now we don't have the sun's light
or its warmth. That's why it's almost
always colder at night than during
the day."

Just then, the outside
lamp came on.
Moth flew towards it.

"I sleep during the day,"
she said, "so I don't see
the sun. But I love
the lamp's light
and its warmth."

Oscar looked up.
He could feel the lamp's
warm light on his face.
"Is the lamp as hot as
the sun?" he asked.

"No," said Moth,
"the sun is our
brightest and
hottest light."

"Are all lights hot?" Oscar asked.

"Not all," said Moth, "but many are."

Oscar climbed off the step and looked out at the starry sky.
Moth flew down to join him. "You can only see the stars
at night," she said…

"They are always shining, but you can't see them in the day because of the light from the sun."

Our sun is a star too. It is closer to the Earth than other stars, so its light is much brighter for us and it looks very big.

Moth flew towards the street.
"Without the sun's light,
we need other lights
to help us," she said.

Oscar could see
the lights of an aeroplane,
a streetlamp and
a light in the window.

"What are those little lights?"
he asked. "They're dancing!"
"Those are fireflies," Moth said. "They are
beetles that can make their own light."

And she told Oscar about how some living creatures make light in their own bodies.

Male fireflies wait till dusk to fly up and show off to female fireflies by flashing light signals.

Malaysian land snails wake up at night and flash green signals to each other.

The sun's light does not reach far into the sea and many sea creatures make their own light.

If anything tries to eat a Swordfish squid, it squirts a glowing ink cloud. This dazzles the hungry fish and the squid can escape.

The rim of a Crystal jellyfish glows green when it is disturbed.

The Californian millipede is poisonous. At night its whole body lights up to warn other animals not to eat it.

The Anglerfish lives in the deep sea. It has a big spine on its head, the tip of which glows blue-green. If smaller fish come to see it, the anglerfish eats them.

"I wish I could glow too," Oscar said.

Just then, Oscar noticed
something swooping about.
"Look, Moth. There's your
shadow!" he called.

"My body is stopping some of the light
from reaching the wall," Moth said.
"It leaves a dark patch
that's the same shape as me."

"Where's my shadow?" asked Oscar.
"If you stand up," Moth said, "you'll see."

Oscar got up.

There was
an Oscar-shaped
shadow!

Oscar lay down again (and so did his shadow).

He closed his eyes.

The dark behind his eyelids made him feel sleepy.

"Is it nearly the morning?" he yawned.

"Not yet, Oscar," said Moth.

But Oscar didn't hear her. He was already dreaming about the bright sun, the shining stars and deep sea fishes.

Thinking some more about light

Talking to Moth, Oscar found out that…

Light comes from many different things.

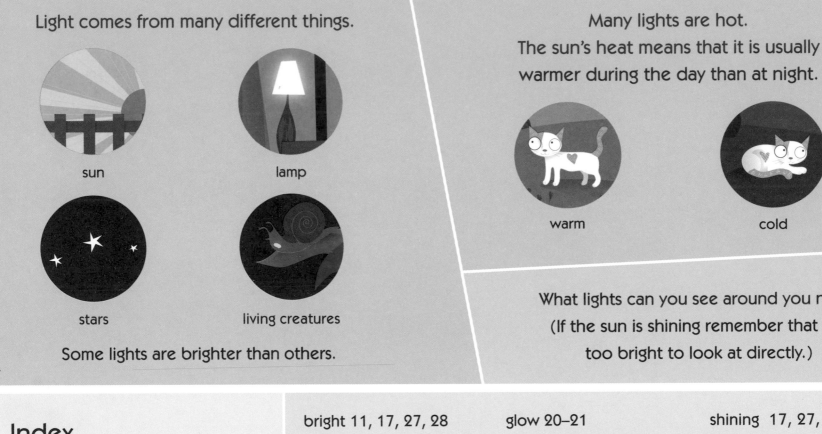

sun

lamp

stars

living creatures

Some lights are brighter than others.

Many lights are hot.
The sun's heat means that it is usually warmer during the day than at night.

warm

cold

What lights can you see around you now?
(If the sun is shining remember that it is too bright to look at directly.)

... and dark

Many lights are easier to see at night.

stars

fireflies

When we don't have the sun's light, we need other lights.

aeroplane lights

streetlamp

When something blocks the light, it makes a shadow.

The dark can make us feel sleepy.

Do you turn off the lights in your bedroom before you go to sleep at night? If you keep a nightlight on, does it make shadows?

Oscar thinks light and dark are great! Do you too?